Alice Meets the Aliens

BY TEDDY SLATER
PICTURES BY ALEXANDRA WALLNER

Silver Press

For Becky Margulies, who's out of this world.
—T.S.

For my friend Alice, who always knows how to
help aliens get home.
—A.C.W.

Library of Congress Cataloging-in-Publication Data
Slater, Teddy.
  Alice meets the aliens / by Teddy Slater;
pictures by Alexandra Wallner.
    p. cm.—(What belongs?)
    Summary: A young girl helps a family of aliens return
home. At various points in the text the reader is asked to guess
what belongs in the picture.
    [1. Extraterrestrial beings—Fiction. 2. Science fiction.
3. Literary recreations.]
I. Wallner, Alexandra, ill.   II. Title.   III. Series.
PZ.S6294Al   1992
[E]—dc20   90-43549
ISBN 0-671-72979-9 LSB   ISBN 0-671-72980-2   CIP
                                                    AC

Produced by Small Packages, Inc.
Text copyright © 1992 Small Packages, Inc.
and Teddy Slater

Illustrations copyright © 1992 Small Packages, Inc.
and Alexandra Wallner.

Published by Silver Press, a division of
Silver Burdett Press, Inc.
Simon & Schuster, Inc.
Prentice Hall Bldg., Englewood Cliffs, NJ 07632.

Printed in the United States of America.

10   9   8   7   6   5   4   3   2   1

Something strange awakened Alice. She sat up in bed and gazed around her room. It looked exactly the way it always looked.

She kicked off her covers and ran to the window. But there was nothing strange outside—just a pale yellow moon, a few wispy clouds . . . and one more thing.

What do you think belongs with the moon and the clouds?

Is it a galaxy of glittering stars,

a great big feather duster,

a bunch of ripe bananas,

or a tiger on a tightrope?

As Alice stood watching, the brightest star in the galaxy
began to fall. It tumbled down to Earth, gleaming like a jewel:
first red, then blue, then red again. Brighter and brighter
the starry thing glowed. Closer and closer it came.

Alice blinked once, then twice, in disbelief.
For there on her lawn was a tiny spaceship!

Alice dashed down the stairs and out into the night.
Slowly the door of the spaceship opened, and three alien
creatures emerged. There was a mother, a father . . .
and one more thing.

What belongs with an alien mother and father?

Is it a chimpanzee
on roller skates,

a graceful ballerina,

a jolly old juggler,

or a young alien child?

The alien child stepped forward. "Good evening, Earthling,"
he said in a voice like the wind. "My name is Xyrkle Gwyrkle.
This is my mother, Myrkle, and my father, Fyrkle. We come from
the planet Zynlox and we mean you no harm.

"Our planet is much like Earth," Xyrkle went on, "but our sky is red and so is our sea. In fact, just about everything on Zynlox is red—except ourselves, of course." He sighed deeply. "Zynlox is a lovely place."

The alien sounded so homesick, and his parents looked so sad,
Alice decided to try and cheer them up. She excused herself
politely, went back into the house, and returned with
some special gifts for her guests. She gave them a bowl of
red ripe cherries, her shiny red yo-yo . . . and one more thing.

What belongs with the red cherries and the red yo-yo?

Is it a gooey hot-fudge sundae,

a bright blue pogo stick,

a bouquet of red roses,

or some polka-dotted pajamas?

Myrkle loved the roses. "How clever of you to give us red gifts," she said. "Maybe you are smart enough to solve our problem as well. You see, we were on our way to Jupiter when Fyrkle made a wrong turn. By the time he realized his mistake, the ship was running low on fuel.

"Luckily, we had enough left for an emergency landing," Myrkle
went on. "But now we're stuck here, without a drop of fuel."
"My dad will give you some gas from his car," said Alice.
But Fyrkle shook his head. "Ordinary liquids will not do.
Only red Zynloxian seawater can fuel a Zynloxian ship."

Alice had no idea where to get red Zynloxian seawater,
but she had to try *something* to help the aliens.
She filled a bucket with water from the garden hose.
Then she went to the refrigerator and got out some
bright red tomato juice . . . and one more thing.

What belongs with water and juice?

Is it a jar of pretty sea shells,

a bottle of raspberry
rhubarb soda,

a wad of chewy bubble gum,

or a sackful of wriggly snakes?

"Try this," Alice said, pouring the water and tomato juice into the fuel tank. But it wasn't enough to get the ship going— nor was the soda, despite its *extra*ordinary flavor. Poor Alice was so disappointed she began to cry. But as her salty tears spilled into the tank, a wonderful thing happened.

Tears, water, soda, and juice all combined to make something
very much like Zynloxian seawater. The ship began to shimmer.
The aliens cheered. "Time for us to go home," said Myrkle.
But before they left, the Gwyrkles took Alice for a quick spin
around the Earth. It was their way of saying thank you.

The spaceship touched down just long enough to let Alice out,
and then it set off for the stars. Alice waved till it was
out of sight. And then she went back to bed.

E
Slater
Alice meets the aliens